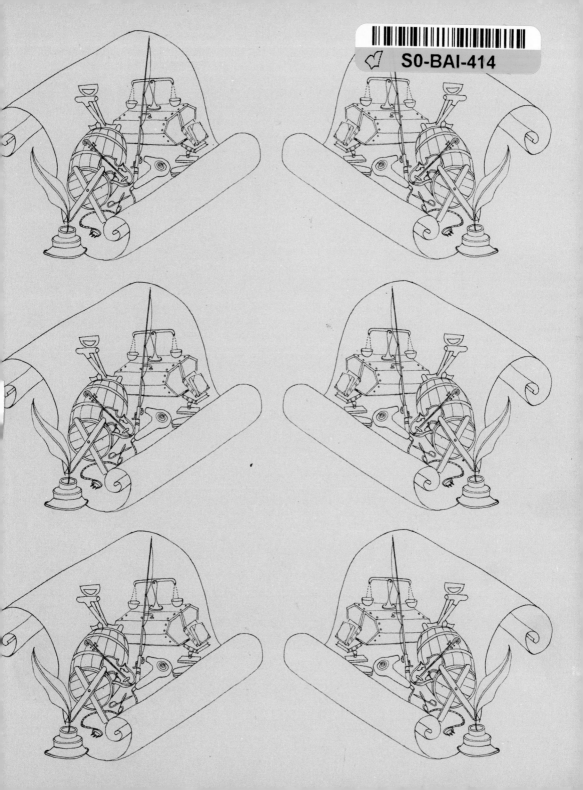

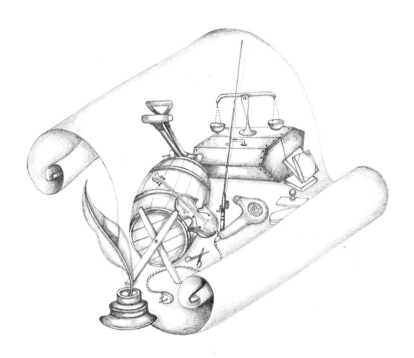

JACK OF ALL TRADES

For Graham

First U.S. edition published in 1985 by
David R. Godine, Publisher, Inc.
306 Dartmouth Street
Boston, Massachusetts 02116

LC 85-70143
ISBN 0-87923-581-0

Calligraphy by Jacqueline Sakwa

aven
PZ
7
.U4158
Jac
1985

Printed in the U.K.

JACK OF ALL TRADES

LIZ UNDERHILL

David R. Godine · Publisher
BOSTON

Young Jack Russell
    popped out of his box:
"I'm a practical pup,"
    said he,
"And old enough now
    to look for a job,
A trade or profession,
    let's see . . ."

FISHERMAN

A fisherman's life is all
    hooks, rods and reels,
And dozens
    of flies to tie;
But have I the patience
    to wait hours and hours
In the hopes of a bite?
    No, not I!

"The Fly Fisherman"   Liz Underhill June 1985

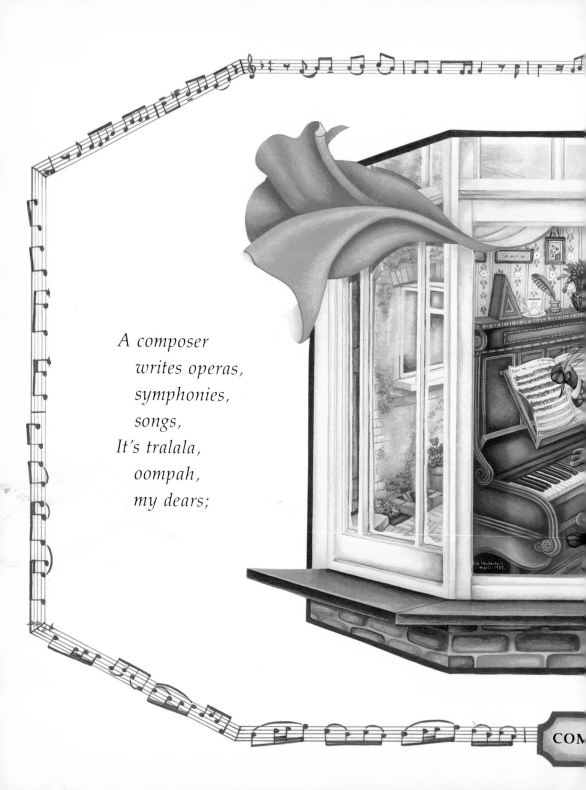

A composer
　　writes operas,
　　symphonies,
　　songs,
It's tralala,
　　oompah,
　　my dears;

COM

I'm a singer already:
BOWO-O-OW
WOW WOW!
Now why
are you
stopping
your ears?

LAWYER

I could be a lawyer
   defending a crook
In front of a judge,
   old and grim:
But if the judge learns
   I'm a bad little pup
He'll put me in jail
   'stead of him.

The Honest Lawyer

DRESSMAKER

A dressmaker needs
  to be careful and neat,
To sew a fine seam
  without flaws;
Could I manage a thimble
  and be just as nimble,
Without sticking pins
  into my paws?

TEACHER

I'd make a good teacher –
I have a loud voice –
My pupils would be
so polite;
Though someone is certain
to point out, alas,
At the moment I can't
read or write.

PLUMBER

If I were a plumber
  I'd have lots of fun
Splashing folks who get
  into my path;
But is playing with water
  a good idea when
The thing I hate most
  is a bath?

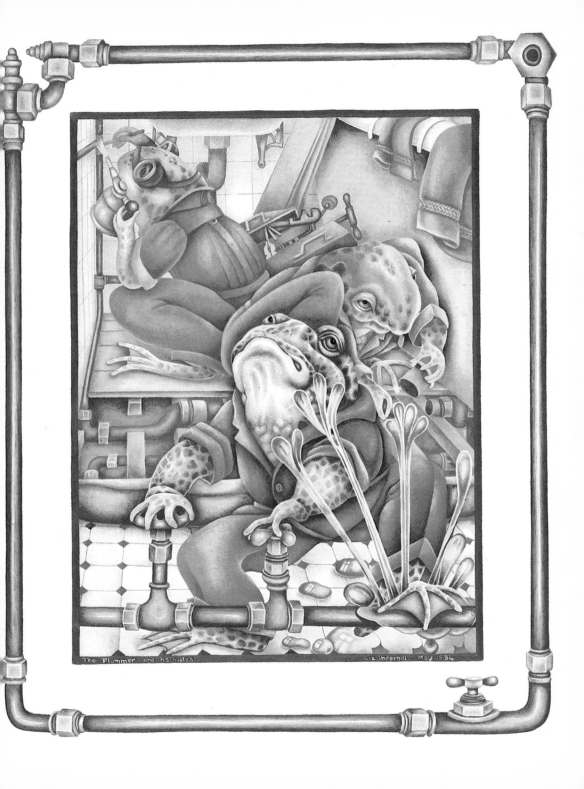

The Plummer and his mates.   Liz Underhill. May 1984.

HAIRDRESSER

A hairdresser sounds
  like a great deal of fun
Such snipping and
  brushing there'd be;
However I'm sure
  I would put up a fight,
If anyone tried
  to brush me!

Chez Monsieur Parrot   Liz. Underhill. June 1984

TOUR GUIDE

As tour guide I'd be
  in charge of young kids
To plan routes
  and help them along,
It's fun when they stop
  to stay for the night
But not to clean up
  when they've gone!

The Hostel Warden   Liz Underhill Aug 1983

A good cleaning lady
must bustle about
Making the house
spick-and-span;
I'm willing to try,
but so clumsy am I
I'd probably trip over
my pan.

The Attendant   Liz Underhill. March 1984

I could work
    in a bank
    and hand out
    the cash
In bundles,
    for any
    amount.

BAN

There's only
    one drawback
    to wreck
    my career:
Jack Russell,
    poor fellow,
    can't count.

GARDENER

A gardener grows
*   all his produce in rows,*
Peas, cauliflower,
*   broccoli, beans,*
And cabbage and spinach . . .
*   but just wait a bit . . .*
Who's heard of a dog
*   that eats greens?*

The Market Gardener   Liz Underhill. May 1984

BARTENDER

Serving beer in a pub
sounds like my kind of job,
As does serving my friends
bread and cheese;
I enjoy all the noise,
cracking jokes with the boys,
But the smoke from cigars
makes me sneeze.

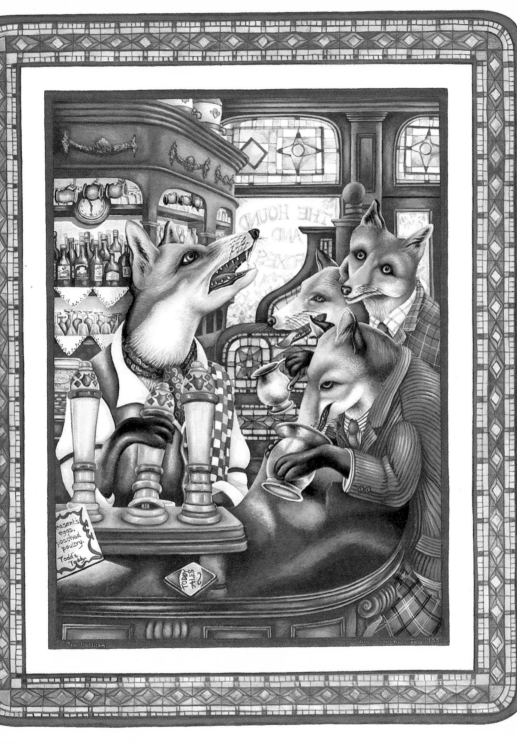

I've made my decision.
  I'm going to bed,
For one thing
  is perfectly plain:
There's one job I love,
  it's the one I do best . . .
It's being
  a puppy again!